KU-104-000

GREAT TALES FROM LONG AGO

DICK WHITTINGTON

Retold by Catherine Storr
Illustrated by Jane Bottomley

Methuen Children's Books

in association with Belitha Press Ltd.

Note: Dick Whittington's story is based on fact. He was Lord Mayor of London for the first time in 1397, and again in 1408 and 1420. The author has used as her sources for the story many historical references, as well as the version published by John Jacobs in his *English Fairytales*. The artist has based her illustrations on a number of books covering the period of Whittington's life, including *Chaucer's England* by Duncan Taylor and *A History of Everyday Things in England* by Marjorie and CHB Quennell.

Copyright © in this format Belitha Press Ltd, 1986
Text copyright © Catherine Storr 1986
Illustrations copyright © Jane Bottomley 1986
Art Director: Treld Bicknell
First published in Great Britain 1986
by Methuen Children's Books Ltd,
11 New Fetter Lane, London EC4P 4EE
Conceived, designed and produced by Belitha Press Ltd,
2 Beresford Terrace, London N5 2DH
ISBN 0 416 53550 x (hardback)
ISBN 0 416 54040 6 (paperback)
All rights reserved. No part of this book may be reproduced or utilized in any form or by any means, electronic or mechanical, including photocopying, recording, or by any information storage and retrieval system, without permission in writing from the Publisher.
Printed by Purnell & Son (Book Production) Ltd,
Paulton, England

COLLEGE OF CANTERBURY CHRIST CHURCH LIBRARY
T
398.22
STO
243143 ED

DICK WHITTINGTON WAS THE SON OF A LANDED GENTLEMAN who lived in the Shire of Glo'ster. Dick was only the third son, and when his father died, he was left very poor. All he had of his own was a cat. People told him that if he went to London, he would be able to make his fortune.

AT FIRST HE DID NOT KNOW
how he could get to London.
But one day he saw a wagon
drawn by eight horses,
passing along the high road.
It was going to London.
"May I go with you?" Dick asked the wagoner.

"You may. But you will have to walk.
There is no room in my wagon
for another pair of breeches," the driver said.
So Dick walked beside the wagon and the horses
all the long road to London,
where he had heard that
the streets were paved with gold.

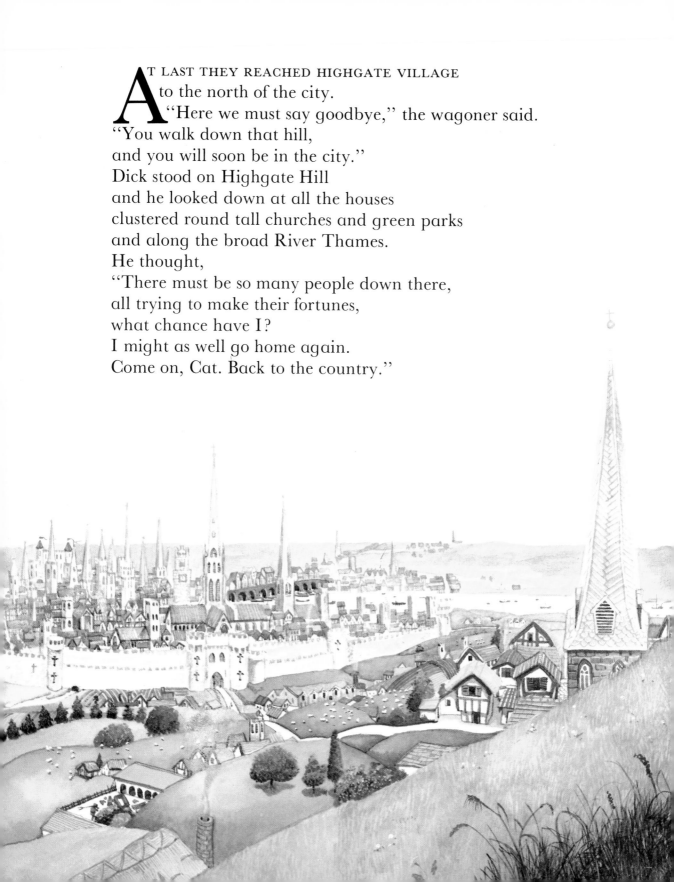

AT LAST THEY REACHED HIGHGATE VILLAGE
to the north of the city.
"Here we must say goodbye," the wagoner said.
"You walk down that hill,
and you will soon be in the city."
Dick stood on Highgate Hill
and he looked down at all the houses
clustered round tall churches and green parks
and along the broad River Thames.
He thought,
"There must be so many people down there,
all trying to make their fortunes,
what chance have I?
I might as well go home again.
Come on, Cat. Back to the country."

He had picked up his luggage
and turned his back on London,
when all the church bells of the city below him
began to ring.
Dick stopped to listen, and it seemed to him
that the bells of St Mary-atte-Bowe were calling to him.

Turn again Whittington,
Thou worthy citizen,
Lord Mayor of London!

"Lord Mayor! That wouldn't be so bad!"
Dick thought,
and he turned as the bells told him,
and went on his way down the hill into London city.

WHEN HE WAS DOWN AMONG THE HOUSES AND CHURCHES,
Dick looked around for the streets of gold.
But all he saw were cobbles and mud and dirt
and crowds of people, too busy to notice him.
He tried to speak to one or two people
to ask where he might find somewhere to sleep,
something to eat, any work he could do.
But everyone was in too much of a hurry to listen.
At last, after several days,
Dick was very hungry and very cold
and without a home.
He found a corner on the steps of a great house in the city,
and there he lay himself down to sleep – or to die.

IN THE MORNING HE WOKE,
still colder, and still hungrier.
At that moment, the door at the top of the steps opened
and he saw a woman come out of the house,
with her hands full of kitchen scraps.
She threw them out to the fowls in the yard.
When she saw Dick,
half asleep on the steps below,
she began to scold.
"What are you doing there, you lazy good-for-nothing?
Get away with you, or I shall call the master."

Just then, her master, Mr Fitzwarren,
a rich merchant, appeared at the door.
He said, "Hold your noise, woman.
Let me hear what this young man has to say for himself."
Then Dick said, "Sir, I am newly come from the country.
I had hoped to find work here in the city
and to have earned my own bread.
But no one stops to listen when I speak."

Mr Fitzwarren was sorry for the boy.
He told the cook to give him as much food
as he could hold and then to find work
for him to do in the kitchens.
"If he is honest and works hard,
he shall not be left to die in the street," he said.

S O DICK FOUND A HOME IN THE GREAT CITY OF LONDON.
He worked hard, and he had food enough.
When he first slept in his attic room,
he thought he would be kept awake all night
by the squeakings and scamperings
of the rats and mice who shared the room with him.
But it took his cat only a day and a night
to get rid of them all.
"What luck," Dick thought,
"that my share of my poor father's fortune was my cat!
I wonder if I shall be as lucky in time to come?"
He thought that perhaps he might;
for his master Mr Fitzwarren was kind to him,
and he knew that Miss Alice,
Mr Fitzwarren's daughter, liked him too.

ONE DAY MR FITZWARREN CALLED
all his servants into his room.
He told them that one of his ships
was soon going to sail to Africa
to trade with the people there.
He asked each man and woman
whether they wanted to send anything in the ship
in the hope of selling it there for a good price,
or if they liked,
they could entrust the captain with money
to buy goods in Africa
which would sell well in England.

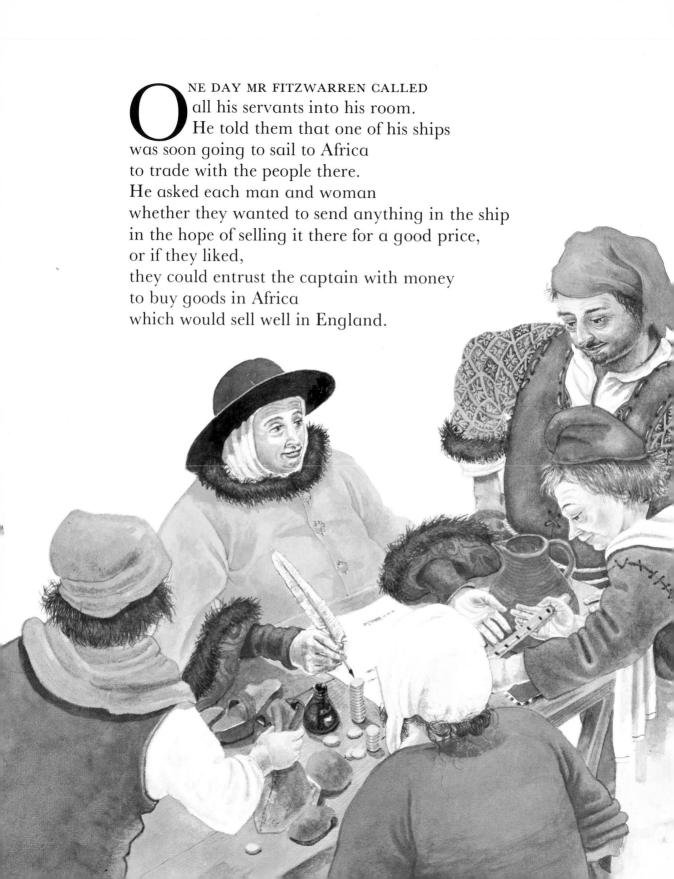

Each of the servants
had something to send with the ship,
except for Dick, who had nothing.
Alice offered to lend him money,
but this he refused.
At last, very sadly, he offered to send his cat,
though he could not imagine
how she would bring him back any return.

AFTER SHE HAD LEFT LONDON,
the merchant ship sailed for days and weeks
till she reached the Barbary coast of North Africa.
There the captain began to trade,
selling the goods he had brought from England,
and buying spices and silk and jewels to take back again.

The King of the country sent for the captain
to show what he had to sell.
When the captain arrived at the palace,
he found the King and Queen trying to eat a splendid meal.
But the tables and floors
were covered with rats and mice,
who leapt boldly on to the King's own plate
and carried off the choicest morsels of food.

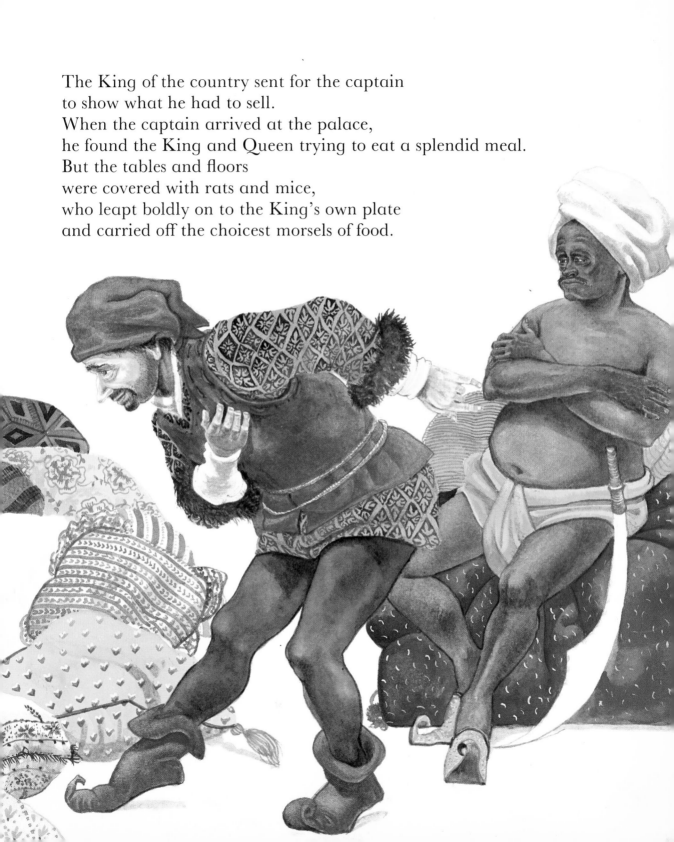

The captain was astonished.
"Your Majesty, why do you allow these vermin
to plague you so?" he asked.
"Alas! We have no way of getting rid of them,"
the King replied.
"Allow me to send to my ship
and I will show you a creature
who can help you," the captain said.
Sure enough, no sooner had the cat
been brought into the palace,
than she leapt on one rat after another,
killed a hundred mice, and in no time at all,
had cleared every room,
so that there was not one of the beasts left.

The King was overjoyed.
He declared that no matter what the price,
he must have the cat for his own.
He ordered his servants
to bring in chests full of precious stones,
jewellery and gold coins
to pay for this rare and precious creature.
The captain, knowing how poor Dick was,
and how sad he had been to part with the cat,
agreed to sell her for this great treasure.
The chests were loaded on to the ship,
the King kept the cat,
and the captain sailed joyfully back to London.

W HEN THE CAPTAIN RETURNED TO MR FITZWARREN'S HOUSE,
he told him the story of the cat,
and showed him the treasures which the King
had sent back for Dick.
Mr Fitzwarren was delighted to hear of the boy's good fortune.
He sent a servant to fetch Dick and said,
"From now on he is to be called *Mr* Whittington."

When Dick came in, Mr Fitzwarren told him
that he was now richer than his master.
"I will help you, my boy
to make the most of your wealth.
We shall soon see you as good a gentleman
as any man in the land," he said.

D ICK WHITTINGTON DID INDEED BECOME A GENTLEMAN
and a successful merchant.
In time he married Alice Fitzwarren,
who had always liked him
when he was still a poor working boy.
He had his own house,
kept a stable of fine horses,
and was Lord Mayor of London,
as the Bowe Bells had foretold, not once but three times.

He was knighted Sir Richard Whittington,
and was rich and grand enough
to lend money to the King of England,
and to entertain him and his Queen
to a magnificent banquet.

And there is still a stone on Highgate Hill
to mark the spot
where young Dick turned back from his journey
to listen to the promise of Bowe Bells.

CANTERBURY CHRIST CHURCH COLLEGE

WHITTINGTON STONE

SIR

RICHARD WHITTINGTON
THRICE LORD MAYOR
OF LONDON
1397 — RICHARD II
1406 — HENRY IV
1420 — HENRY V
SHERIFF — IN 1392

THIS STONE WAS RESTORED
BY E. HILLIER
1935